BY
Lynn Plourde

PAJAMA DAY

ILLUSTRATED BY
Thor Wickstrom

Dutton Children's Books

New York

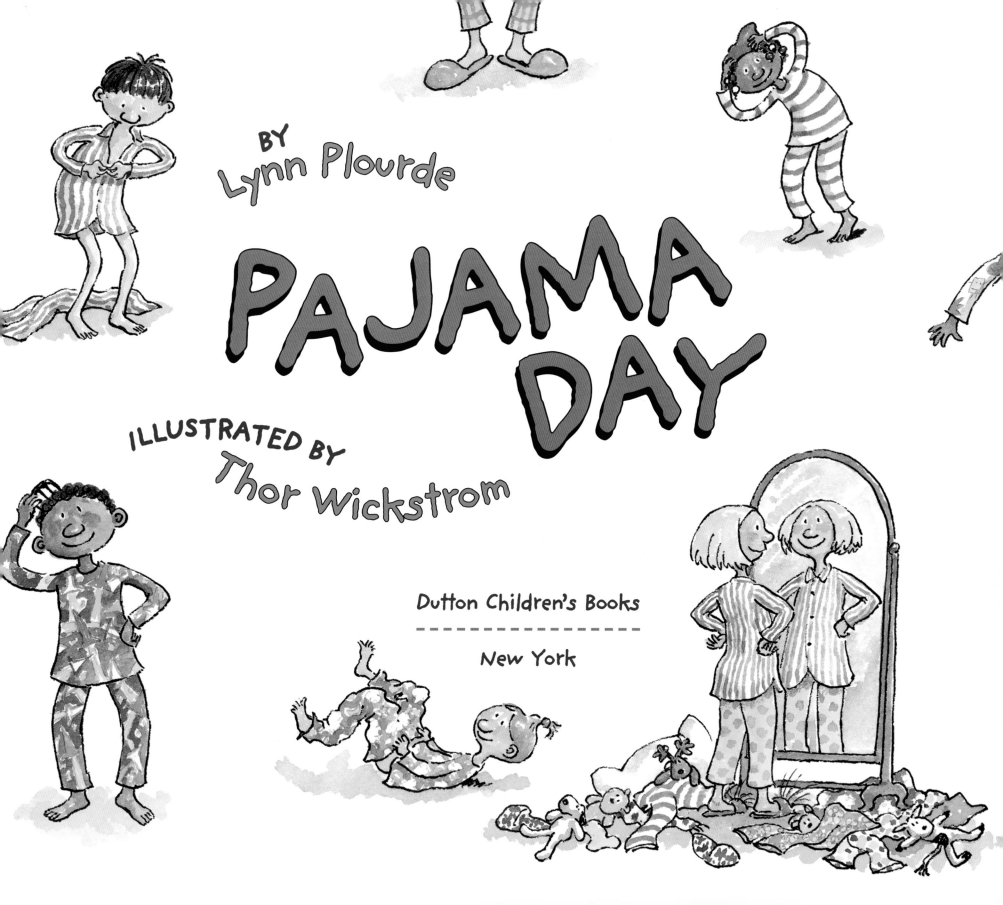

With love to Krista,
who is *never* forgetful but always creative
—L.P.

To Michele, with love
—T.W.

ON'T
GET
NG!

DON'T
FORGET
PJ'S!!

REMEMBER:

Text copyright © 2005 by Lynn Plourde
Illustrations copyright © 2005 by Thor Wickstrom
All rights reserved.

CIP Data is available.

Published in the United States by Dutton Children's Books,
a division of Penguin Young Readers Group
345 Hudson Street, New York, New York 10014
www.penguin.com

Designed by Irene Vandervoort
Manufactured in China   First Edition
ISBN 0-525-47355-6
10 9 8 7 6 5 4 3 2

It was Pajama Day at school, and everyone in Mrs. Shepherd's class arrived wearing their favorite fuzzy-wuzzy PJ's.

Everyone, that is, except . . .

Drew A. Blank.

Drew had forgotten what day it was. In fact, Drew might have forgotten his own name if it hadn't been written on his hand as a reminder.

Mrs. Shepherd greeted everyone: "Welcome, class. Slide off your shoes and slip on your slippers to join us at our morning meeting circle."

"Oh, fudge, I forgot my slippers," said Drew. "I knew there was a reason I tied a string around my finger."

"Don't worry, Drew," said Mrs. Shepherd. "You can join us anyway."

Drew didn't want to be the odd man out,
so he rummaged in the lost-and-found pile.

After diving and digging and
pulling and tugging . . .

... Drew joined the circle wearing slippers.

Later that morning, Mrs. Shepherd said, "Snack time, everyone. Get out the breakfast snacks you brought for Pajama Day."

"Oh, double fudge—I forgot mine," said Drew. "I knew there was a reason I stuck a sticky note to my stomach."

"Don't worry, Drew," said Mrs. Shepherd. "I'm sure someone will share with you."

Drew didn't want to be the odd man out,
so he asked if he could go see the cook in
the cafeteria.

Drew and the cook found
some flour, sugar, eggs, and milk.

After stirring and whisking and frying and flipping . . .

. . . Drew went back to his class with an extra-special breakfast snack for everyone.

Next, Mrs. Shepherd announced, "Hurry, class. Time to line up for the Pajama Parade."

"Oh, triple fudge—I forgot to wear my pajamas," said Drew. "I knew there was a reason I wrote *PJ's* on the top of my homework assignment sheet."

"Don't worry, Drew," said Mrs. Shepherd. "Just go to the craft corner and find something to decorate your shirt. You can join the parade when you're ready."

Drew didn't want to be the odd man out, so in the craft corner he found some cloth, yarn, glue, and glitter. After clipping and snipping and drizzling and sprinkling . . .

... Drew joined the parade just in time.

Right after lunch, Mrs. Shepherd said, "Time to perform our teddy bear play. Everyone, get out your favorite teddy bears and get in your places."

"Oh, quadruple fudge—I forgot mine," said Drew. "I knew there was a reason I drew a big *T* on today's date on the calendar."

"Don't worry, Drew," said Mrs. Shepherd. "You can be in charge of the curtain."

But Drew didn't want to be the odd man out, so he found a furry friend and went over to the dress-up corner.

After buttoning and zipping and combing and crowning . . .

DRESS-UP CORNER

. . . Drew and his friend joined the play. And he was a big hit.

Later that afternoon, Mrs. Shepherd said, "Now it's silent-reading time. Everyone, grab a book from the shelf and the pillows you brought from home and get cozy."

"Oh, quintuple fudge—I forgot my pillow. I knew there was a reason why I set the alarm on my wristwatch—so I'd remember it."

"Don't worry, Drew," said Mrs. Shepherd. "Just roll up your sweater for a pillow."

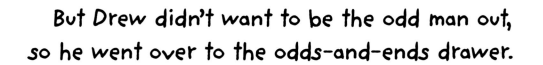

But Drew didn't want to be the odd man out, so he went over to the odds-and-ends drawer.

After huffing and puffing and twisting and tying . . .

. . . Drew joined the rest of the class with a pillow.

At last, Mrs. Shepherd's class settled down for silent reading.
Everyone snuggled up on their pillows and opened their books.

And soon the only sound coming out of Mrs. Shepherd's class was

Z-Z-Z-Z-Z-Z-

Z-Z-Z-Z

After curling up with their pillows and books, and getting all comfy and cozy, everyone snoozed.

Everyone, that is, except . . .

Drew A. Blank.

Drew tossed and turned and fussed and fidgeted. He couldn't sleep. He had the nagging feeling he was forgetting something.

What is it? thought Drew. *What am I forgetting* this *time?*
He checked his strings, his sticky notes, his "To Do" list...

What could it be? Drew worried.

Drew tossed and turned one too many times on his pillow
and . . .

Mrs. Shepherd and all the other students woke with a start.

"Yikes! What was that?"

"Ow—that hurt my ears."

"Hey, who woke me up?"

"Wh-wh-where am I?"

"Sorry, everyone, my pillow popped," said Drew.
"I was trying soooooooo hard to remember something."

Mrs. Shepherd looked at her watch and said,
"Why, thank you, Drew, for waking us. It's time
to go home, everyone. Hurry or you'll miss the bus."

Mrs. Shepherd's students grabbed their teddies, books, and pillows and raced out to the bus.

But as Drew started to scrunch his toes into his socks, he noticed a note written on the bottom of his foot:

Don't take the bus.
Mom will pick you up
after school today.

Drew wiggled his toes at Mrs. Shepherd. "See, that's what I was trying so hard to remember."

"Well, now you know, Drew," said Mrs. Shepherd. "But why's your mom picking you up today?"

But before Drew could draw a blank, his mother arrived. "Oh, thank you, Mrs. Shepherd, for making Drew wait for me. There's not a minute to waste. Let's get going, Drew."

"First, there's your piano lesson. Then your dentist appointment. Then soccer practice. Then the Scout meeting. Then . . ."

Later that night, Drew plopped onto his bed, all pooped out from Pajama Day. As a matter of fact, he was so pooped out that he forgot . . .

to put on his . . .

PAJAMAS!